STEPHEN MICHAEL KING

YOU

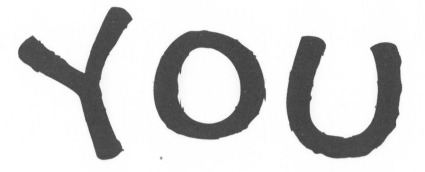

A Story of Love and Friendship

 GREENWILLOW BOOKS
An Imprint of HarperCollinsPublishers

You: A Story of Love and Friendship

Copyright © 2010 by Stephen Michael King

First published in 2010 in Australia by Scholastic Press, an imprint of Scholastic Australia Pty Limited.

First published in 2011 in the United States by Greenwillow Books. This edition published under license from Scholastic Australia Pty Limited.

All rights reserved. Manufactured in China.

For information address HarperCollins Children's Books,

a division of HarperCollins Publishers,

10 East 53rd Street, New York, NY 10022.

www.harpercollinschildrens.com

Watercolor and ink were used to prepare the full-color art.

The text type is Goudy Old Style.

Library of Congress Cataloging-in-Publication Data

You / by Stephen Michael King.

p. cm.

"Greenwillow Books."

Summary: Reveals the world as a colorful, musical, and exciting place
where the most special thing of all is a best friend.

ISBN 978-0-06-206014-3 (trade bdg.)

[1. Best friends—Fiction. 2. Friendship—Fiction.] I. Title.

PZ7.K58915You 2011   [E]—dc22   2010032237

11 12 13 14 15 SCAU 10 9 8 7 6 5 4 3 2 1

First Edition

 Greenwillow Books

The world is a colorful place—

yellow,

red,

blue,

and all other colors.

The world is colored with big things,

small things,

and all sorts of things.

But the most colorful part of my world is . . .

YOU.

ting

The world is a musical place,

with high notes,

low notes,

and all the notes in between.

But the most musical part of my world is . . .

YOU.

The world is an exciting place,

with ups,

downs,

around and arounds,

and far, far aways.

But the most exciting place in my world

is with . . .

YOU.